The Mini-Brick City

Story by Carmel Reilly
Illustrations by Alan Brown

Contents

Chapter 1

The Class Challenge

Every Monday morning, Mr West gave his class a special challenge.

"This week, you will use plastic mini bricks to make parts of a city," he said. "You can work in pairs. Each pair will make a building or a place in the city."

Jayden and his friend Devin were delighted about this challenge.
They loved working together.
And they loved making things with mini bricks.

Mr West began to tell each pair
what he wanted them to make.
The city would have a town hall,
an airport and a train station.
There would be city buildings,
stadiums, parks and playgrounds, too.

"I'd really like to make the football stadium,"
Devin whispered to Jayden.

Soon, Mr West called out their names. "You two will make the city's roads," he told them.

"Roads are not very exciting,"
Devin grumbled to Jayden.

"Don't worry," said Jayden. "Let's just start building some and see what happens!"

Devin fetched a box of mini bricks.
He poured them onto a mat on their table.

Jayden began snapping together lots of grey bricks
into a long stretch of road.
Devin added a row of white bricks
to make a line down the middle.

Chapter 2

Not Just Roads

After a while, Jayden stood back to look at what they had made. "I feel like there is something missing," he said.

"Buses are important in cities," said Devin. "We could add some bus lanes."

"That's a great idea!" said Jayden. "And we should make some bicycle lanes, too. That will make the city much more eco-friendly."

Over the next few days, Devin and Jayden worked hard.
They made long, wide roads for the outside of the city.
And they made smaller streets for the middle of the city.
They used green bricks to make the bus lanes
and blue bricks for the bicycle lanes.

Suddenly, Devin said, "Do you know
what we have forgotten to make?"

Jayden stared at the roads for a few seconds.
"Oh! Footpaths!" he said.

Chapter 3

A Special City

Soon, it was the end of the week.
One by one, everyone in the class
put what they had built onto the big table.

"See how tall that tower is!" said Devin.
He pointed to a building Josie and Stella had made.

“And Essie and Alex’s football stadium is great,” said Jayden, looking a little worried. “Everything looks much more exciting than our roads.”

Just then, Mr West said to Devin and Jayden, “Now it’s your turn to show us what you have made.”

Devin and Jayden looked at all the buildings on the table. "We could start by putting one of our streets in between the town hall and the school," said Devin.

The boys began snapping mini bricks into place. Carefully, they laid down roads between other buildings. They added the bus lanes, bike lanes and footpaths, too.

"Look!" said Mr West, when they had finished.
"The roads have turned our buildings into a real city."

Mr West held something out to each of the boys: a mini-brick bus and car!

“You two brought our special city together,” he said. “Would you like to be first to drive around it?”

“We would *love* to!” Devin and Jayden said together.